Little
Brown
Bushrat

For my little sisters, Annabel and Holly,

because I'm so proud of them both.

First published in 2002 by Macmillan Children's Books
A division of Macmillan Publishers Limited
20 New Wharf Road, London N1 9RR
Basingstoke and Oxford
Associated companies throughout the world
www.panmacmillan.com

ISBN 0 333 96082 3 HB
ISBN 0 333 96083 1 PB

Text and illustration copyright © 2002 Georgina Ripper
Moral rights asserted

3 5 7 9 8 6 4 2

A CIP catalogue record for this book is available from the British Library.

Printed in Belgium by Proost.

Georgie Ripper

Little Brown Bushrat

MACMILLAN CHILDREN'S BOOKS

As the sun shone down on the dusty red earth of the Australian outback, a little brown bushrat made his way home.

On the way, he came
across a group of animals
talking loudly. They were
busy discussing what it was
that each of them did best.

"I am by far
the most beautiful,"
said the lyrebird,
and he displayed
his magnificent
tail feathers.

"I can jump higher than anyone
else," said the kangaroo,
as she cleared
a particularly
tall bush.

"I can hang upside down
by my tail," said the possum
and they all agreed that
no one could possibly do that
quite so well.

"Well, I can run the fastest,"
said the emu, and he ran
round and round the clearing
very fast indeed.

Bushrat was amazed. He couldn't run very fast, or jump very well and, despite what his mother said, he didn't think he was very beautiful. He was also pretty sure that if he tried to hang upside down by his tail, something very nasty would happen.

One by one, the other animals spoke up.

The rainbow lorikeet
was the most colourful.

The duck-billed platypus
was the best swimmer.

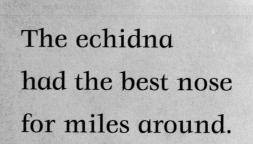

The echidna
had the best nose
for miles around.

Even the lazy koala
could sleep for longer
than anyone else.

Bushrat sighed miserably and wiped away a tear.
"I'm just a scrawny little brown bushrat
who's no good at anything,"
he thought to himself.

He was wandering sadly off into the bush when
suddenly he heard a commotion behind him.

He turned around to see the wompoo fruit dove
come bursting into the clearing.
"Fire!" she squawked.

"Fire!"

Everyone was silent . . .

and then . . .

The kangaroo jumped up and down.

The emu ran round and round in circles.

The stress was all too much
for the lazy koala who promptly
fell asleep.

Only one animal managed to keep calm.
The little bushrat sniffed the air
and followed his nose towards the fire.

He found it in a small clearing where
the hot sun had set fire to a pile of dead leaves.
It was only a little fire, but as every bush animal
knows, the smallest fire will very quickly turn
into a raging bushfire if it is not put out.

Through the trees he could see the river. Bushrat
thought for a second and then leapt into action.

He started digging . . .

and digging . . .

and digging . . .

until, just when he thought
he couldn't dig any more . . .

Whoosh!

Bushrat broke through the river bank
and the water flooded out.

The strong current swept him off his feet
and he only just managed to grab hold of
an overhanging twig before the water gushed
into the clearing.

Tired and wet, Bushrat climbed
down the branch and wandered
back to the clearing.

The water had put out the fire
and one by one the other
animals returned. The possum was
the first to speak. "Bushrat saved us.
He's the bravest animal in the
whole bush."

And how they all cheered and cheered.
The little bushrat glowed with pride.
"I'm the bravest!" he thought.

Hooray! Hooray!

That evening, with the cheers of the other animals still ringing in his ears, Bushrat smiled to himself. "I am the best at something after all," he thought. "I just didn't know it."